'**Watch out**, people, here they **come**,
They are the gang with the big bare **bum**.

Ring that bell,
CLANG CLANG CLANG,
That's why we call them the
BARE BUM GANG.

They're like something off the **telly**,
They're all bare and they're all **smelly**.'

Coming Soon:

THE BARE BUM GANG BATTLE THE DOGSNATCHERS

www.barebumgang.com

THE BARE BUM GANG

and the
Football Face-off

ANTHONY McGOWAN

Illustrated by Frances Castle

RED FOX

THE BARE BUM GANG AND THE FOOTBALL FACE-OFF
A RED FOX BOOK 978 1 862 30386 7

First published in Great Britain by Red Fox,
an imprint of Random House Children's Books
A Random House Group Company

This edition published 2008

3 5 7 9 10 8 6 4 2

Text copyright © Anthony McGowan, 2008
Illustrations copyright © Frances Castle, 2008

The right of Anthony McGowan to be identified as the author
of this work has been asserted in accordance with the Copyright,
Designs and Patents Act 1988.

The Random House Group Limited supports the Forest Stewardship Council
(FSC), the leading international forest certification organization. All our titles
that are printed on Greenpeace-approved FSC-certified paper carry the FSC
logo. Our paper procurement policy can be found at
www.rbooks.co.uk/environment.

Set in Bembo MT Schoolbook

Red Fox Books are published by Random House Children's Books,
61–63 Uxbridge Road, London W5 5SA

www.kidsatrandomhouse.co.uk
www.rbooks.co.uk

Addresses for companies within The Random House Group Limited can be
found at: www.randomhouse.co.uk/offices.htm

THE RANDOM HOUSE GROUP Limited Reg. No. 954009

A CIP catalogue record for this book is available from the British Library.

Printed in the UK by CPI Bookmarque, Croydon, CR0 4TD

To the BBG originals:
Graham Doran, Simon Morley
and Niall McGowan

Chapter One

HOW IT STARTED

It all started when Jennifer Eccles said she wanted to be in our gang. Until then we were just called *the Gang*.

The people in the Gang were:
- Ludo, that's me;
- Noah, my best friend, who we sometimes call Doc;
- Jamie;
- Phillip, usually known as The Moan, because he is always moaning, who has the bad luck to be Jennifer's brother.

As well as names, we all have jobs in the Gang. Of course I am the Gang Leader, which means they all have to do what I tell them, except quite often they don't.

Noah is the Gang Doctor, which is why we sometimes called him Doc. Gang Doctor is quite an important job. Noah has to carry dock leaves around with him for when someone gets stung by nettles. And if you get a grass cut, which is when you pull some grass and it cuts you, he has to wee on it. Weeing on it is all you can really do for a grass cut, which everyone knows is the worst thing that can happen to you.

Noah's mum is a nurse and she told him that wee hasn't got any germs in it, and that it's better for washing bad injuries than using water out of a puddle. But it's quite hard for Doc, because he might not want to have a wee exactly when you get a grass cut, so you have to stand around for a bit while he makes himself, by thinking about waterfalls and running taps and babbling brooks.

Jamie is our Gang General, which means he takes charge in Times of War. He got the job because he's the best at throwing stones and fighting, even though he isn't actually very good at throwing stones or fighting, just better than the rest of us.

The Moan – I mean Phillip – is the Gang Admiral, which is a bit silly, as we don't have any ships. We had a bit of an argument about it. The trouble was that we all had cool jobs except Phillip, who wasn't anything when we started. So he said:

'I'm going to be the Admiral.'

'Don't be stupid,' I said. 'We haven't got a navy.'

'Well, that doesn't matter,' he replied sulkily. 'We *might* get one. We could expand and take over someone else's navy.'

I didn't know of any other gangs nearby who had a navy we could take over, but I didn't say anything.

'He could be in charge when we play Bomb the Bismarck.'

That was Noah speaking. He was always being nice and trying to stop arguments.

Bomb the Bismarck, by the way, is when it rains and there's a gigantic puddle and you put a big stick or a plank to float in the puddle and then you throw stones and bricks at it until it sinks or surrenders. It's probably the best game you can play that involves a puddle, a plank and some stones.

Well, that's our gang, and we didn't want Jennifer or any sister or any other type of girl to be in it. Everyone knows that girls are rubbish at being in gangs and get you to tidy up your gang den and try to make your action figures wear dresses. A girl in a gang is like a stone in your shoe, or a hair in your throat, or a bit of bird-poo in your ice cream.

But she just wouldn't take no for an answer. She used to follow us around and it really spoiled things, having her miserable face wherever you looked. So that's when I said to her:

'Look, Jennifer, there's a special test you have to pass to be in our gang.'

I didn't know what the test was going to be when I said that, but I knew I'd be able to think of something. I was good at thinking of things, which is why I was Gang Leader.

'What test?'

Jennifer had her suspicious face on. It was like her normal miserable face but more suspicious looking. Her hair was sort of banana-coloured, and it was tied in a kind of knot-thing on top of her head, with more hair squirting out of the top of it, so it looked a bit like yellow lava exploding out of a volcano.

'Just a test. A *special* test.'

'I don't believe you.'

'Well, you should. There *is* a test. You don't know anything.'

'OK then, I'll take your stupid test. What do I do?'

I did some hard thinking, expecting a bright idea to pop into my brain. But nothing popped, so I decided to play for more time, which is something even famous geniuses need to do occasionally.

'First we have to go to the den.'

We were at the park. The park has some broken swings, a broken roundabout, a broken seesaw and some grass, which would probably be broken as well, if you could break grass. Next to the park there is a football pitch. It has some proper goals but, like everything else, they are broken, because someone stole the crossbar from each one. What the thief wanted with two crossbars is a bit of a mystery. Maybe they needed some replacements because someone stole *their* crossbars.

Anyway Noah was there with us – I mean, me and Jennifer – but not Jamie or The Moan.

'Go and get the rest of the Gang,' I said to Noah. 'Meet us at the den.'

Chapter Two

THE DEN

The den was in the tiny bit of a wood that's left between the new estate and the old estate. We live in the new estate and most of our enemies live in the old estate.

All the way there Jennifer kept nagging at me to tell her what the test was. And when I didn't tell her, she started to guess.

'Do I have to walk in bare feet over broken bottles?'

'No.'

'Do I have to eat worms?'

Good idea that, but I didn't want to do

it after she'd said it, because that would be copying.

'Er, no.'

'Do I have to set fire to the school?'

'Don't be stupid. Your mum would tell the police and the whole gang would be put in jail.'

'Do I have to eat mud?'

'No.'

'Do I have to eat your bogies?'

'No. It doesn't involve eating *anything*.'

Maybe I shouldn't have said that. It cut out an awful lot of tests, such as eating leaves, eating pepper, eating a raw sausage, etc., etc.

'Does it involve spiders?'

'No.'

'Does it involve any creepy crawlies?'

'No, not really.'

She leaped on that, like a lion attacking a zebra.

'What do you mean "not really"? Do you mean it does *a bit* involve creepy crawlies? Or don't you even know?'

She could be quite logical sometimes, which you don't really expect from girls, or at least from girls with volcanoes coming out of the tops of their heads.

'I'm not answering any more questions until we reach HQ.'

HQ stands for Head Quarters, which is another way of saying our den. We'd built about six dens in the woods, because the kids from the old estate kept smashing them up or burning them or doing wees in them so they smelled.

Our latest den was quite well disguised with grass on its roof, and it was half dug into the side of a little hilly thing, and there was a weeping willow tree draped over it. The grass roof was over a sort of extension made of old planks sticking out from the side of the hill. I sometimes used to wish that our enemies were looking for us from a helicopter gunship, because from a helicopter gunship it would be impossible to see us.

The door was a plastic sack that once contained cement powder, and it usually managed to sprinkle a bit of the grey stuff on your head when you pushed through on the way in.

'OK, we're here now,' announced Jennifer, as if she was already in the Gang and the den belonged to her.

'Excuse me,' I said, 'but it's *my* job to say when we're here.'

Jennifer looked at me like I was mad for a while. Her looking-at-me-as-if-I-was-mad look was a lot like her normal grumpy look, except her eyes were wider, and her mouth made the shape of a chicken's bottom.

I think it might have been the chicken's bottom that gave me the idea, although the idea itself didn't arrive for a few minutes as it had to sit and stew in my brain for a while before it was ready.

There was an embarrassing silence for about three minutes, although I didn't have a watch so it might have been four minutes or maybe just two. Then I said:

'Let's go and sit in the den until the others get here.'

Jennifer looked a lot happier when I said that. She'd never been allowed in the den before. I realized straight away that I'd made a big mistake. I should have done the test outside. I imagined how hard it would be to get her out of the den again once she was in. If she created a rumpus, she might do quite a lot of damage. We had valuable things inside, like some bendy bamboo, some other less bendy sticks, a cricket bat, two cricket stumps, a bicycle inner tube, some string and some more string less tangled up than the first lot of string. And we had some matches.

Even if she didn't mess up our sticks or our string, Jennifer might kick a hole in the wall – the wall at the front, I mean. The other walls were made out of the hill, so it would be hard to destroy those without a bulldozer.

'It smells in here,' she said, which really annoyed me.

13

'What of?' I was a bit worried that our enemies might have found this den too, and done some wees in it.

'Earth. I like it.'

I groaned. That was the last thing I wanted to hear. If only she had said, 'It smells of wee in here, and I'm never coming in again,' then all our troubles would have ended.

There was another embarrassing pause and then I heard the rest of the Gang arrive, and Phillip pushed his head through the door and gave a loud groan when he saw his sister.

'Why don't you just get lost?' he said.

He was always the rudest one to Jennifer, because she was his sister. I sometimes thought he went a bit too far. But he was also slightly afraid of her because she was the same height as him, even though she was a year younger.

Jennifer stuck out her arm with her palm two centimetres away from Phillip's face.

'Say it to the hand,' she said.

Noah, who had come in behind Phillip, said, 'That's a sign of yob culture. If that's how you're going to behave, you might as well go and join the old estate gang.'

Jennifer hung her head and said, 'I don't want to join them. I only want to be in your gang.'

I felt a bit sad then. But I'd already had my idea, which was now nicely cooked and ready to be served. Once Jamie was in the den – and, yes, it was a bit of a tight squeeze, if that's what you're thinking – I began.

'As you all know, Jennifer wants to be in our gang.' The Moan moaned and Jamie groaned, and even nice Noah made a little tut. 'Well, as you also know, before anyone gets to be in our gang, they have to do The Test.'

I checked the boys. Yes, they were all in on the trick – Noah had warned them, although they didn't know *exactly* what to expect.

'It's what is called an Initiation Ritual.'

Chapter Three

THE TEST

There was a gasp. I'd seen a programme on the telly once where a man went to live with a tribe in Africa or somewhere, and before he was allowed to join in with the hunters he had to have a wooden spike shoved through his cheeks. I think he might have had another spike stuck somewhere under his trousers, but the camera didn't show that bit. It was horrid, and he nearly cried, even though he was a grown-up. I wasn't intending to do *that* to Jennifer, but I did remember that it was called the Initiation Ritual, which made it sound very important.

Jennifer now began to look slightly afraid, although she couldn't have known about the spikes as the programme was past her bedtime. Jennifer looking afraid was mostly like the normal Jennifer, except more afraid.'

'Do you still want to go through with this?' I asked, trying to make my voice go all deep and scary.

'Yes,' said Jennifer, but there was a quiver in her voice.

'Right. The only way anyone gets to join the Gang is if they show us their bare bum. So *that's* what you've got to do.'

A fair bit of pandemonium broke out then. Noah exploded into a spluttering laugh; Jamie went, '*Yeeeuuoughghghghgh,*' and I thought he was actually going to be sick; Phillip lived up to his name with what was probably the biggest moan ever heard in the history of the world up till then, although I suppose someone in India or China or somewhere might have done a bigger moan that wasn't recorded.

Anyway, all that fuss wasn't quite what I'd wanted, because it might make Jennifer realize that this wasn't our usual Initiation Ritual. In fact up till now our Initiation Ritual had been me saying to people, 'Do you want to be in my gang?' and that was it.

So I tried to cover it up by doing some more talking.

'Well, there you have it. The Test. The Initiation Ritual. No bare bum, no in gang. Sorry, but that's the way it is. Rules are rules.'

Jennifer stared at me with the sort of look you'd use if you opened your presents on Christmas morning, and instead of a PSP or a new mountain bike, you found a My Little Pony, complete with a pink grooming comb. I mean, it was a look that blended together shock and horror.

That was all fine, exactly what I'd planned, confirming me as a genius.

It was then that Jennifer should have shouted at us for a while, and then crawled off, never to bother us again. And the first part of that seemed to be working. Jennifer turned round and began to shuffle towards the door. But then she stopped and turned round again to face us.

'OK then,' she said, a look of grim determination on her face.

There was a sort of wail of dismay from the others.

'W-what?' I said.

'If that's what I have to do, then I'll do it.'

And before anyone could stop her, Jennifer Eccles pulled down her frilly pink knickers and showed us her horrible white bottom. It looked like a jellyfish, one of the dead ones you see on the sand at the seaside. And just like with a dead jellyfish, even though you know it can't really hurt you, it was still pretty scary.

If the very mention of Jennifer's bum earlier on had set off a riot, what happened now was ten times worse. At school we did the Blitz, when German bombers completely blew up London, and it was exactly like that in our den. We all dived for cover, trying to hide from the killer-jellyfish bum, but it was like the eyes in that painting that seem to follow you all around the room, and we just couldn't escape from it.

Finally Phillip managed to scream, 'Get out, get out, and take your disgusting bum-cheeks with you.'

'No way,' said Jennifer. 'I'm in the Gang now, and there's nothing you can do about it.'

I had to get this sorted out, and quickly.

'Look, Jennifer,' I said in my most grown-up voice, 'I'm sorry, but you can't be in the Gang. The Gang is boys only, and that's the way it has to stay. Please go now. But let's shake hands first, so everything's nice and, um, civilized.'

I stuck my hand out towards her. But then my hand began to tremble like a leaf in the wind. Because, you see, I was looking at Jennifer's face, and it wasn't pretty. I mean, even more unpretty than usual. She'd begun to change colour. First she went white, and then there were red spots on her cheeks, and then the spots joined up and her whole face turned a bluey-purple colour, a bit like when there's about to be a massive thunderstorm. And suddenly Jennifer began to look larger. She was quite big to begin with – like I said, she was as tall as Phillip, and Phillip was taller than me. But now she seemed to be expanding in all directions. If she'd been a cartoon, then steam would have come out of her ears, but as this was Real Life, it didn't.

'I think she's gonna blow,' said Noah.

I tried to push some of our sticks and string out of her way towards the back of the den with my foot.

And then I saw a glistening in her eyes. Oh no, this was the worst thing that could happen – she was going to cry. I'd almost have preferred it if she had smashed up our best bits of bamboo, or even the whole den, than this. I didn't like making people cry, especially girls. If I liked making girls cry, I'd have spent more time hitting them, or calling them Fatty and Five-Belly-Nelly, or the other things they don't like. I knew I'd played a rotten trick on Jennifer, and when you do something rotten, you feel rotten.

'It's OK,' I said, 'there's no need to cry. I'm sure there are lots of other gangs you could join. They're probably just as good as our gang.' I didn't mean that bit, but everyone knows it's OK to tell lies when you're trying to stop girls from crying. 'Some of them probably allow girls in already. They'd probably let you make their sandwiches. Maybe a bit of dusting around their dens. Too much dust can give you asthma . . .'

Then I sort of trailed off, because something even weirder was happening to Jennifer. Weirder, I mean, than the changing-colour thing she was doing. She was beginning to shake. At first I thought this was part of the crying, which meant it was going to be a massive sobbing fit, and I felt like a really bad person for causing so much misery.

But then I realized that she wasn't crying at all.

She was laughing.

To begin with she laughed so hard she couldn't speak, but then she calmed down a bit, so she could get it out.

'Ha-ha-ha-ha-ha-ha-ha! To be in your gang you have to show your bare bum! You're the Bare Bum Gang, *that's* who you are. The Bare Bum Gang. And nobody knows. Well, they'll all know now, because I'm going to tell them! *Bare Bum Gang, Bare Bum Gang, Bare Bum Gang.*'

And with that she turned herself round yet again, and crawled out through the door.

But that wasn't quite the end of it. Before we'd even had time to take it all in, we heard a muffled banging sound, and then the extension part of the den fell in, and we saw Jennifer outside, still laughing, but not so hard that it had stopped her from kicking the living daylights out of our HQ.

Chapter Four

THE BAD NEWS SINKS IN

'That was rubbish,' said The Moan. 'I can't believe we let you be Gang Leader. If it was up to me you'd be Gang Toilet Cleaner. In fact I wouldn't even let you do that because you'd be rubbish at it.'

Luckily my best friend, Noah, came to the rescue.

'That's not true. He'd be a really good Gang Toilet Cleaner, if we had a toilet. It's not Ludo's fault that Jennifer wanted to be in the Gang. It's your fault for having such an annoying sister.'

'That's not fair!' The Moan replied. 'It's not like you get to choose. No one ever said to me, "What would you like, a really cool older brother, who can teach you how to make a brilliant bow and arrow and lend you his pen knife, or a stupid sister, who'll ruin your gang and kick your den in?"'

'OK, everyone calm down,' I said. I knew it was now that we needed a true leader, and it had to be me. It was my great chance to shine. 'Let's take a good look at the problem.'

'We all know what the problem is,' said Jamie. 'The problem is that when we go to school on Monday, every single kid is going to know that we are in a gang called the Bare Bum Gang, and that you have to show your bare bum to be in it. They're all going to laugh so much they'll puke up their Turkey Twizzlers.'

'We don't have those any more,' said Noah.

'Well, their vegetable pasta bake then.'

'But that's only if Jennifer tells them,' I said.

'And how are we going to stop her?' Noah asked reasonably.

'Yeah,' said The Moan, 'she's already told us she's going to blab. And I don't blame her. Why did you have to say all that bare bum stuff?'

'I just thought she'd say no, and that would be it. But that's all in the past now. I have an idea.'

'Oh no,' said The Moan. 'Any more of your ideas and the Gang will be finished.'

I ignored him. 'I think there's a way we can stop her from talking.'

'How?' asked Noah.

'We let her into the Gang.'

'Are you mad?' said Jamie. 'She'll never join us, not now we're the Bare Bum Gang. Who would? Only some loony who liked showing his bare bum.'

'Or *her* bare bum,' added Noah.

'Don't call us the Bare Bum Gang!' I said

sharply. I really didn't want the name to take hold, even in our heads. 'I think she'll jump at the chance. It's what she's always wanted.'

'No way!' said Phillip, shaking his head. 'If she's in, I'm out. It's bad enough having to see her at home. And anyway, what would she be? It was hard enough thinking up a decent job for me to do.'

'I thought, perhaps, she could become Gang Doctor,' I said quietly.

There was a stunned silence. I sneaked a quick glance at Noah. He looked like he'd been stabbed in the back, which was true, sort of. But being a Great Leader means you have to make tough decisions.

'B-b-but *I'm* Gang Doctor,' he said, and I thought he might blub, which would have been embarrassing for all of us.

'Look,' I said, in a kind sort of way, 'there are lots of lady doctors, but there aren't any lady admirals or generals. We'll think of a new job for you.'

'I like being Doctor, said Noah, getting angry. No one had ever heard him shout before. 'And you can't have a girl as Gang Doctor. Everyone knows that girls can't wee in a straight line. They wee all over the place. Jennifer would be useless at fixing grass cuts. We'd all die of gangrene before she managed to wee on the right spot.'

'What's gangrene?' asked Jamie.

'It's when you get a grass cut, or even some other kind of cut, and first your finger turns green, and then your hand, and then your whole arm. Then, if they don't amputate your arm, which means chopping it off, the rest of you turns green and you die in terrible pain.'

There was a hushed silence as the awful reality of having a girl Gang Doctor sank in. This wasn't going well.

'But she could carry the dock leaves OK, that's not so hard,' I said. I was clutching at straws, or rather dock leaves.

'That's only half the job,' said Noah,

growing in confidence. 'And you have to know where to find them, and even if you do find some, they quite often grow right next to nettles, so you have to be brave to pick them. If you ask me, it would make more sense to have Jennifer as Gang Leader than Gang Doctor.'

The Moan moaned, and Jamie said: 'Now you've gone too far. We don't want her in at any price and that's that.'

So that was the decision. We'd just wait to see what happened on Monday. We weren't little kids any more. We'd tough it out, we'd see it through.

Chapter Five

THE HORROR, THE HORROR

'So, you've got a stomach ache *and* a headache?'

I nodded.

'And you feel sick?'

'Mmmmm.'

'And you think you've got a temperature?'

This time I was too ill to do anything except close my eyes, the way you would probably do if you were about to die from malaria or the plague, or when gangrene spreads to your whole body.

'And your arm hurts?'

'And my leg too.'

'Which one?'

'Both of them.'

I opened my eyes again and saw that Mum was smiling, which was bad news.

'Up you get.'

I got to school late and so did Noah, Jamie and The Moan. They'd all tried pretending they had terrible diseases too. The Moan still had some faint red marks where he'd used his mum's lipstick to draw measles on his face. Jennifer wasn't with him. She must have come to school early.

We met up just outside the school gates.

'Maybe it'll be OK,' I said hopefully.

'We're all doomed,' said Jamie.

I looked at The Moan, who should have known best, as he had to live with Jennifer. He didn't say anything. Just shook his head sadly. That was enough to tell us what would be waiting for us later on.

The morning turned out to be fine.

No one mentioned anything about bare bums, although I did think some of the girls looked at us in a funny way. The worst moment came when Miss Bridges asked me a question and I made a silly reply and then she told me off for being cheeky. Delilah Jones giggled behind her hand, and I thought it might be because, you know, bums have cheeks. But then Delilah just went back to her work, so I thought I was probably imagining it. It looked like the full story hadn't got out yet.

But then came morning break. As soon as we left our classroom and walked into the playground, we knew our lives were going to get much worse. The whole of Jennifer's Year Four class were lined up in a row. Their faces were shining with a nasty sort of joy. As soon as we appeared, they all pointed at us, their fingers jabbing like daggers, and they started singing a stupid song. It went like this:

'Watch out, people, here they come,
They are the gang with the big bare bum.
Ring that bell, clang clang clang,
That's why we call them the Bare Bum Gang.
They're like something off the telly,
They're all bare and they're all smelly.'

The words weren't very clever, and the tune was rubbish, just a sort of a droning noise, but that didn't matter to the crowd that gathered. Jennifer was in charge, and she danced around in front of the others, conducting the choir and sometimes leaning forward with a nasty expression to sing the words extra loud.

As if things weren't bad enough, that's when Dockery arrived. Dockery is massive. His neck is thicker than my waist and when he makes a fist, his hand is as big as a cannonball. He looks about three years older than anyone else in the school. One funny thing about him is that although he has a gigantic head, his face — I mean, his eyes, nose and mouth — are all tiny and squished up together in the middle of it.

I wish I could say that he was a gentle giant who liked to pick wild flowers and look after sick puppies but he was just a big bully. He was also spoiled rotten, and had a PlayStation 3, an Xbox, a Game Boy Advance, a Nintendo DS and a PSP. He has a load of friends who hope one day he'll let them play with all his stuff, but he never does.

So there was Dockery, with his gang. Oh, I should say, they were also the gang from the old estate who used to burn down or wee on our dens whenever they found them. So from now on I'll just call them the Dockery Gang. As well as Dockery; there was William Stanton, James Furbank, Paul Larkin and some others whose names I could never remember. They were mainly in Year Six.

To begin with they joined in with the song, but they soon got bored with that. So then Dockery came over and pushed me down and then sat on me, and then he shouted to his friends, 'Right, if this is the Bare Bum Gang, let's see their bare bums!'

He was sitting on my chest and it really hurt. I saw Jennifer out of the corner of my eye, and she had stopped leading the other kids in the song, and she wasn't looking crazed any more. In fact she looked a bit sad, probably because she wanted to do all the teasing herself and didn't like anyone else getting in on the act. She ran off, and the rest of the choir scattered, but Dockery was still sitting on my chest.

Luckily, before they managed to pull my trousers down Miss Bridges appeared.

'What's going on here?' she said in a strict voice.

'Nothing, miss,' said Dockery. 'We're just playing, aren't we, Ludo?'

'Yes,' I mumbled. I didn't have much of a choice. Then Dockery got off me.

'See you later,' he said as he and his gang walked off.

'Are you OK?' asked Miss Bridges.

'Fine,' I said, looking at my feet.

'There's nothing you want to tell me?'

'No, miss.'

I should have told her that Dockery was a big bully, but he'd have got me for it later.

No one really bothered us for the rest of the break, except that every now and then one of Jennifer's class would come up and say 'Bare Bum Gang' and then run off.

Jennifer didn't say anything. But at lunch break I saw her doing cartwheels. She could do one after the other, and the only thing that stopped her was reaching the wall at the end of the playground. Even though I thought that was quite cool, it still seemed like she was only doing cartwheels because she was so happy about getting her revenge on us.

Chapter Six

SMARTiES-TuBE FART BOMBS, ETC.

We all met up in the den that evening after tea to talk things over. We had to fix up the extension bit first, but that didn't take us long. The damage looked worse than it was. The Dockery Gang would have made a much better job of wrecking the den, not to mention the weeing-on-it part.

The earth inside the den was always nice and dry, even when it was raining outside, and we also had an old dog blanket and some newspapers on the floor, so compared to most dens it was a palace. Noah had some fizzy fish and Phillip had some crisps. Mum had given me some raisins but I was too embarrassed to get them out. Raisins are OK if you're on an expedition and there's nothing else to eat for miles around, so you'd starve without them, but apart from that they aren't much use. Noah shared out the fizzy fish, but he kept the red and black ones for himself, which we agreed was probably fair.

'That could have been much worse,' I said when we were all settled. I meant the day of teasing and being sat on by Dockery, not the destroyed extension.

'Yeah,' said The Moan, 'we might have been squashed by a steamroller and then chopped up into bits and then flushed down the toilet. That might have been worse. A bit.'

'No need to be sarcastic,' said Noah, loyal as ever.

'I'm going to have nightmares for the rest of my life about it,' said Jamie. 'All

I'll hear is "Bare Bum Gang, Bare Bum Gang" for ever.'

I said, 'Well, it was pretty embarrassing, but it should die down now, don't you reckon, Phillip? She won't go on for ever, will she, your sister?'

'You don't know my sister. Once, when I annoyed her, she threw all my Airfix models out of my bedroom window. I was watching the telly downstairs, and at first I didn't realize what it was. Just saw these streaks out of the corner of my eye. Then I looked properly, just as my last Spitfire bit the dust.'

We all quietly absorbed what The Moan had said. There were obviously no depths to which the evil Jennifer would not stoop. But then something happened that, for the time being, put all thoughts of the Jennifer problem out of our minds.

The first thing we heard was a loud rattling noise, the second was a yelp and the third was a voice crying out,

'Poooooooooooooooooh!'

The traps!

I should explain about our traps. Because our dens kept getting discovered and smashed in or weed on, we invented some traps to catch anyone who came near. There were two sorts of trap. The first sort was a hole dug in the ground and then covered over with sticks and bits of other stuff to hide it. The Moan wanted to put broken glass in the bottom, or nails pointing up, or sharpened wooden stakes, but Noah said that was barbaric, which means bad, so we didn't. Instead we put either nettles, dog poo or Smarties-tube fart bombs in them.

You make a Smarties-tube fart bomb by farting into a Smarties tube, which takes quite a lot of skill. Then you quickly put the top back on the Smarties tube to keep it in. The idea of the Smarties-tube fart bombs is that the fart gas becomes really strong and horrible by being stored for a long time in the Smarties tube. Then, when one of our enemies steps on the trap, they burst open the Smarties tubes, and the fart gas, by now really, really poisonous, floats up and suffocates them, but not to death – just enough to make them sick, so they run away home.

In case you are wondering what a Smarties tube is: well, back in the olden days, Smarties used to come in a special round tube, with a cool lid that you could pop off and on. When I was little, I used to eat quite a lot of Smarties, and I always saved the tubes, because I knew they'd come in handy one day, either for farting into or for keeping other sweets in, like Jelly Tots or wine gums. The new kind of Smarties tube has eight sides and a cardboard lid. They don't really work very well for keeping farts in, because they aren't airtight or, rather, fart-tight, as they have too many holes and the fart gas leaks out. I suppose you could use them in an emergency, but they wouldn't be very potent. If you haven't got a load of old, proper Smarties tubes, you could use Pringles tubes. Obviously, they take a lot more filling up, as each one can hold up to four big farts, eight medium-sized ones, or twelve tiny little tummy squeaks.

Anyway, altogether there were six of these pit traps around the den – three nettles (because they were the easiest), two dog poo and one Smarties-tube fart bomb, because they were the hardest to make, and my supply of Smarties tubes was getting low.

The other kind of trap was what is called a snare, which is a piece of string or wire made into a loop. When one of your enemies puts his foot in the loop, it tightens and they are trapped. Jamie wanted to tie the other end of the string or wire to some bricks high up in a tree, but yet again Noah said we couldn't, because it was barbaric and you might bash someone's brains out, and then you'd go to jail. Also, it would be hard to get the bricks up into the tree, because we were all rubbish at climbing trees, except Noah, who wouldn't do it because of what he said about it being barbaric.

So I had the brilliant idea of attaching the other end of the noose to a load of old tin cans that we took out of the recycling bin. That was a bit of an adventure in itself, because during the expedition The Moan fell into the bin and cut his hand on a sharp edge and, what was worse, got covered in manky old baked-bean juice. He didn't need any stitches, but his mum had to put the biggest plaster in the whole packet on it – the giant oblong one.

Once we had the cans we made holes in them, using a hammer and a nail, and then tied the snares to them, using about six cans for each snare, and then we hid them really carefully around the den.

I knew at once that the rattling noise was the sound of someone stuck in a tin-can snare.

The Gang all looked at me, waiting for a decision. Should we stay in the den to see what happened next? Or should we go out and face whatever was there?

'Come on,' I said. 'We'd better find out what we've caught.'

Chapter Seven

THE CHALLENGE

We crawled out through the cement-bag door and came face to face with our worst fears. Dockery was there with three of his gang. Dockery had got stuck in a tin-can snare and was shaking his leg about, trying to get it free, and that was rattling the cans like mad. His gigantic head and tiny face were glowing bright red. One of his gang, the one called Larkin, who was tall and skinny as a lamppost, had put his foot in one of the pit traps and was waving his hand in front of his face, which had gone a pale green colour, a bit like mint ice cream.

That could have been a Smarties-tube fart-bomb trap or just the dog-poo trap, because they were both quite smelly.

But we couldn't really enjoy the success of our traps, because there was a good chance we were going to get bashed, and that's never very cheerful.

When Dockery saw me, he stopped looking mad and started laughing.

'Ha, look what we found! It's the Bare Bum Gang and their cosy little den. Oh, correction, I mean *our* cosy little den.'

'It's not your den,' I said. 'It's *our* den. We built it. There's plenty of room in these woods. Why don't you go and make one of your own?'

Dockery came stumping up towards me, sticking his jaw out. The cans rattled and clanked behind him, but he didn't seem to notice them.

'We want this one,' he said.

I was frightened of Dockery. He was older and bigger than me, and so were his friends. But I knew that bullies are usually cowards, so I made myself say, 'Well, you can't have it.'

'Yeah, get lost, Dockery,' said Jamie, backing me up.

I was glad we had him as our General. And I felt Noah and The Moan close in behind us. I was a bit worried that they might just run away, but they hadn't.

I didn't want to chicken out, but I also didn't want to have to get into a scrap with Dockery, because fighting is stupid and, anyway, we'd probably lose and get mashed.

Then I had one of my ideas.

'We'll play you for it,' I said.

I don't know why I said that. It must have come from some bit of my brain I wasn't paying attention to.

'What at, tiddlywinks? Flower pressing? Or showing off your bare bum?'

There was a burst of loud rough laughter from Dockery's friends.

'No, er, football.'

'Oh no,' said Noah, and there was another mixture of moans and groans from the other two. Dockery wasn't very good at football, but he made up for it by playing really *really* dirty. Nobody was allowed to get past him – if you tried, he just hacked you down. And his friends were the same, except some of them were also quite skilful. Plus they were all older and bigger than us. Which, taken all together, made it a bit stupid of me to say we'd play them at anything, especially football.

'Football? Yeah, any time you want,' said Dockery, sneering. 'Tell you what, get a team of you new estate kids together, if you can, and we'll massacre you all.'

'Fine,' I said. It sounded a bit like I was saying 'fine' to being massacred, but that's not what I meant. I certainly didn't think it was fine. What I thought was the opposite of fine.

'Great,' said Dockery, and he looked like someone who'd just lost a penny and found a pound. 'Let's make it next Saturday, so you can practise. Not that it'll do you much good. Seven a side. On the field by the park. At three o'clock. If you don't turn up, we'll just come straight here and move into our nice new den, thanks very much. Or, I don't know, maybe we'll burn it. I like to watch things burn.'

Larkin chuckled, and a streak of drool came out of his mouth. It reached halfway to the ground before he sucked it back in. He was good at drooling, Larkin.

'We'll be there, don't you worry,' I said. I didn't like the thought of our best ever den going up in flames. I'd rather they just played in it like we did.

'Oh, *I'm* not worried. *You* should be.'

'We ought to play in different colours,' I said.

'Yeah, I'll tell you what, we'll wear blue and you wear white. White for surrender. White for cowards.'

And then they all went off, laughing and mucking about. Except that Dockery forgot about the cans, and they tangled up in his legs and he fell over. That was the best thing that had happened since this whole story began. It took him about five minutes to get free, and he used some bad words I'd never even heard of.

'Nice work,' said The Moan quietly when they were finally out of range. 'That's the den gone, for sure. We might as well burn it ourselves. We've got the matches.'

'Don't be such a defeatist,' said Noah (he knew lots of good words). 'We should look on the bright side. The other kids from our estate aren't all as rubbish at football as we are.'

'We're not even that bad,' said Jamie. 'Ludo once scored a goal at school.'

He was right. The ball hit the back of my head by accident while I was daydreaming, and flew into the goal.

'It doesn't matter how good we are,' said The Moan, 'Dockery and his lot will never let us win.'

'Well, we can try our best,' I said. 'And at least we can say that we didn't just let them take our den without a fight.'

And then we all went home, feeling about one per cent hopeful and ninety-nine per cent depressed.

Chapter Eight

RECRUITMENT

We had four days to find and train a team of red-hot players, fit to take on and beat the bully boys of the Dockery Gang. There's a film I saw once called *The Dirty Dozen*, where an army captain has to find a bunch of soldiers for a deadly mission, and because it's so dangerous, he has to get them from the army jail, and they're all smelly and dirty, and don't do what they're told. But then he makes them into really good soldiers, and they complete the mission, except for the ones who get blown to bits or shot with machine guns.

I was able to watch it because Mum and Dad went out and we had a babysitter called Tracy, and I told her I was allowed to stay up until eleven o'clock and watch whatever I wanted.

So, finding our team was a bit like that, except we weren't really smelly and dirty, and there was less of a chance of getting blown to bits. The trouble was that the kids on the new estate were mostly younger and more wimpy than the old estate kids. That was because the old estate had been there for longer, so the kids had more time to grow.

We began looking for the three recruits we needed the next day at school. Some kids we asked said yes until they heard who we were going to play against. Then they changed their minds, because they knew that there was no way we could win, and the best thing we could hope for was only getting slightly bashed.

But in the end we did manage to get

a couple of the kids from Year Three, who didn't know what they were letting themselves in for. They were actually quite good. One was called Luke and the other was called Oliver, but I never got it quite fixed in my head which one was which, because these small kids all look the same. The downside of Luke and Oliver was that they only had tiny little legs and so couldn't run very fast, and they were so weak they looked like they'd fall down if Dockery even coughed in their direction.

But, like I said, they were actually quite skilful, which was more than you could say for some of the others we looked at. Most of them didn't even know which way to run, and just sort of milled around, tripping over their feet or getting distracted by the lines on the pitch. And if the ball came near them, they ran away or flapped at it the way you would at a wasp attacking your ice cream.

There was one Year Six boy called Vincent who said he would play for us if we let him be in charge of our gang. Vincent's teeth were green and brown and his hair was so greasy he could squeeze it into whatever shape he wanted – say, a horn or a spiral – and  it would stay like that, and he smelled of smoky-bacon-flavour crisps, which is good if you're a crisp, but bad if you're a person (the same goes for prawn cocktail and cheese and onion). Vincent was good at football, and not just because nobody wanted to get too close to him in case they got a noseful of smoky bacon, or hit with the wet slap of his greasy hair.

We discussed letting him in.

'I don't think we should let him play,' I said.

'That's because you don't want him to be our leader,' replied The Moan. 'You want to stay Leader yourself.'

'I don't want Vincent to be our leader,' said Jamie. 'I couldn't stay in the den at the same time as him. We'd all end up smelling of smoky bacon.'

'I don't want him as Leader either,' said Noah. 'I like having Ludo as Leader. He doesn't even smell a *bit* of smoky bacon.'

'Well,' said The Moan, who was obviously looking for an argument, 'he sometimes smells of something worse.'

'No I don't,' I said. 'What could be worse than smoky bacon? For a person, I mean.'

'Flowers,' said The Moan, looking smug.

He could really fight dirty sometimes.

'That's because of the soap my mum buys.'

'It's girl soap,' he said.

There was a pause while we thought about this. If it was agreed that I used girl soap, then that would be me finished as Gang Leader, and Vincent would take over and we'd all smell of smoky bacon, even if we managed to keep the den, which was not very likely.

It was Jamie who came to my rescue, which I didn't expect.

'That's stupid,' he said. 'Soap is just soap. It's not like lipstick. You don't wear lipstick, do you, Ludo?'

'Only at weekends,' I said.

'He's only joking,' said Noah, which was true.

We told Vincent that he couldn't play because he didn't live on the new estate. We didn't mention the smoky-bacon thing.

Chapter Nine

PRACTICE MAKES PERFECT

The next evening, although we were still one player short, we practised really hard. I organized the training. We began by running round the field by the playground. We were helped in this by Trixie. Trixie was an extremely vicious Jack Russell terrier. She belonged to an old woman called Mrs Cake, who lived in a bungalow next to the pitch. Footballs were always getting blasted into her garden, so she hated all children. As soon as she heard the sound of laughter, she'd drag Trixie out of her bungalow and throw her over the fence, shouting out, 'Get them, girl.'

Trixie was quite an old dog, but she could still run at exactly the same speed as an average child, so she would chase us round and round the field, never getting any closer, never falling any further behind. After twenty minutes Trixie would have had enough, and she'd slink off through a gap in the fence. I often thought that it was a good job Trixie was the size of a large rat, because if she'd been any bigger, she would have eaten maybe three or four children every week.

Normally, of course, being chased by Trixie was a bad thing, but when you're trying to reach peak fitness for a big match, it's exactly what you need. After the twenty minutes was up, we had a lie down, and then practised other football skills, like kicking (the football, I mean), shouting 'Pass! Pass!' and then more kicking.

We ended up by practising taking penalties, in case there was a penalty shootout. We decided that Jamie should go in goal,because he had some gloves. They weren't proper goalkeeping gloves just some woolly ones his granny had knitted for him. One of the gloves had six fingers and the other one had four, because

his granny had something called dementia, which is a disease that makes you count up fingers all wrong. I suppose there might have been some logic to it because altogether there were the right number of fingers, just divided up wrong.

Jamie complained about being the goalkeeper, but he didn't want to lend his gloves to anyone else, so he was stuck with the job. During the penalty practice he didn't let in a single goal, which sounds like he must have been a good choice for goalie until you find out it was really because every penalty missed the target completely, except for mine, which dribbled to a stop before it reached the line.

'Let's just hope it doesn't go to penalties,' said The Moan, and we all agreed.

Chapter Ten

A SURPRISING PROPOSAL

Later that evening, after tea, there was a knock at the door. We have a bell, but about two years ago it got stuck while it was ringing and it rang for two days before the battery ran out, and it hasn't worked since. I was watching a DVD called *Great Footballing Bloopers*, all about funny things that had gone wrong during football games. I had a notebook and a pencil and I was making notes about things not to do, like blasting the ball into your own net, jumping into the crowd to kick spectators who had said mean things about you, head-butting other players right in front of the ref, etc., etc.

'It's for you, Ludo,' said Mum.

I went to the back door. It was a boy I didn't really know called Carl.

'Can I be in your team for the big match on Saturday?' he said.

This was rather strange, because Carl, although he lived on the new estate, quite often hung around with Dockery. He was big and lanky and he was one of the best players in the school team. His hair was always hanging over the side of his face, so you could only ever see one eye. That made him look a bit shifty, but I always thought you shouldn't judge people by how they look. You have to take into account other things, like whether or not they smell of smoky bacon, and also how nice they are.

'What do you want to be in our team for?' I asked back. 'We're probably going to get marmalized, you know.'

'I can't stand Dockery,' he said. His one visible eye wasn't looking at my face but at the middle of my chest. 'He's always boasting about things. He never shuts up about how great he is and how he's got every single decent toy that's ever been invented. Whatever you get for your birthday or Christmas, he always says, "Yeah, I've got that already." And he never lets you play with them.'

'That's true,' I said. 'OK then. We're having our last practice session tomorrow.'

'You should call it a training session, not a practice session,' said Carl. 'Calling it a practice session makes it sound stupid, like you're practising the violin or something.'

I didn't really like the way he said that, sort of sneering. But he was probably right. 'Training session' did definitely sound a bit more sporty. And I didn't want to put him off. With Carl on our side we actually had a small chance of not getting massacred.

'OK, come tomorrow after school for the *training* session.'

Chapter Eleven

Tactics

I did my best to avoid Dockery the next day at school. At morning break I saw him and his gang playing football in the playground. They were kicking the ball around to each other. They weren't that good, just big and strong, and they could kick the ball really hard. You could hear the ball hit the brick wall at the end of the playground with a *WHHHAAAANNNG* noise that made your head hum.

The funny thing is that there were only six of them, including Dockery. I wondered who their seventh player was.

At lunch time Dockery saw me in the dining hall (which was just the school gym at lunch time) and sort of smirked at me, which I didn't like, although being smirked at is much better than being bashed. I don't think he was very worried about losing the bet.

The Bare Bum Gang thing still raised its ugly head now and then, but, as Noah pointed out, in a couple of years nobody would remember it, and in a hundred years we'd all be dead anyway, which was a funny way of cheering us up. I think he gets some of his ideas from his dad, who is quite often depressed, which means sad when you're a grown-up.

Jennifer didn't even bother talking to us any more, which suited me. But I still noticed how good she was at cartwheels. I thought about trying one myself, but I was worried it might turn into a disaster, with me in a heap on the floor. That's the thing about cartwheels – you don't even have the faintest idea whether or not you can do them until you try. And when you try there's a very good chance that you're going to look stupid. It's amazing they ever got invented, really.

In the afternoon Miss Bridges asked me if anything was wrong. I said I had a lot on my mind, which made her smile. I wish Miss Bridges was going to be our teacher next year as well, and not that horrible old bulldog, Miss Parks.

We met up before tea for the last practice – I mean *training* session before the big match. I thought it was better to meet before tea, because the last time we were all a bit full, and that slows you down.

Carl was there waiting for us, and he had his own ball, the same kind they use in the Premiership. He was doing keepy-uppy. It looked like he could go on doing it for as long as he liked. My record for keepy-uppy is three.

Trixie wasn't there to begin with, so we

didn't do as much running round the pitch as usual. Instead we did more skills-based training. We practised passing the ball and dribbling, and then we had a rest and drank some water while I had a think about tactics and positions and other important things.

Carl didn't really join in with any of this, because he was already brilliant at the things we were practising. He mainly watched us and sometimes made a suggestion. I felt a bit funny with him watching us like that. It made me more useless than ever, and Jamie and The Moan weren't much better.

Carl laughed at Jamie's gloves, and I thought he was going to go home, but he didn't.

I was pleased with Oliver and Luke, who were really excellent at passing and dribbling. I decided to put them in midfield, where they could do most of the work. Carl would play up front, and the rest of us would be the defence, as all we were really good at was getting in the way, and that might be quite useful if we were getting in the way of their attackers.

'We're going to be playing three-two-one,' I said when I'd worked it all out.

'Eh?' said Jamie.

'The Christmas-tree formation. Three at the back – that's me, The Moan and Noah – two in midfield that's Luke and Oliver – and one up front – that's Carl.'

'What about me?' said Jamie. 'Why don't I get mentioned?'

'I don't know why, but they never count the goalie when they talk about the formation.'

'Well, I don't care. Unless you include me I'm not playing.'

I heard Carl sniggering at this.

'Fine, we'll be playing one-three-two-one. It's still sort of a Christmas tree, but now Jamie is the wooden bit at the bottom.'

'The trunk,' said Noah.

'More like the pot,' said Carl, and sniggered again underneath his floppy fringe.

And that's how our final practice — I mean *training* session ended. Not brilliant, but not a disaster yet, either.

Oh, I forgot, it *did* end in disaster. Because Trixie finally discovered us then (she'd probably been having a nap), and came pelting out and chased us all off the pitch, except for Carl, whom she ignored. The Moan fell down, and Trixie started snapping all around him. She'd never actually caught anyone before, and she was very excited. She looked like a wolf suddenly shrunk down to miniature size.

'Play dead,' shouted Jamie.

'No, that's for when you get attacked by bears,' said Noah. 'Get up and run for it!'

'No, play dead. They don't eat dead things.'

'Don't be stupid,' I said. 'They eat dog food, and that's dead.'

But then Trixie got bored with attacking The Moan and, after a final growl and a quick woof, she went back home. It was probably the best day of her little doggy life.

Chapter Twelve

THE STASH GETS SPLIT

'You look very excited,' said Mum.

It was eight o'clock on Saturday morning. I was pacing up and down in the hallway, carrying my football. Normally at that time I'd be watching TV. Saturday mornings were one of the few times I could watch TV without being hassled by Mum about it.

'Do I?'

I probably wouldn't have used the word excited. I might have said nervous, or maybe scared to death. I was carrying the football because part of me thought that if I could just touch it for long enough, then I might get slightly better at the game. Another part of me knew that was stupid.

'Is something happening today?'

We'd discussed telling our parents about the Big Match. Noah was in favour of it. He said that they would come to support us, and that would mean we wouldn't get kicked around too much by the Dockery Gang, and we probably wouldn't get bashed or squished or pushed around after the game at all. Those were definitely good things – I mean, not getting kicked, etc.

But there was one big thing on the other side of the balance. If our parents came, then Dockery would say that we had to get our mummies and daddies to come and look after us, poor ickle wickle babies deedums deedums.

I'd rather get thumped than have to listen to that, and Jamie and The Moan agreed with me. So we outvoted Noah.

'Nah, nothing, Mum,' I said, back in our hallway. 'We'll probably kick a ball around later on.'

That was true, sort of. I didn't like telling lies to Mum, which meant I spent a lot of time trying to put things the right way.

About half an hour later Noah came round. Sometimes we didn't need to ask to know what the other one was thinking. I could tell from his face that he was as worried as me. We had some toast together in the kitchen. Noah's parents were quite nice but they sometimes forgot to give him meals, so he often ate at our house.

After the toast we went and collected Jamie and The Moan and went to the den. Just then it seemed like the best den in the world, safe and dry and brilliant in every way. It made us all sad.

'This might be the last time we ever get to hang out in here,' said Jamie.

Usually I'd have made a speech about how things weren't so bad, but I didn't have it in me today. I think me not saying anything was a bit of a shock to the Gang. Maybe that's why Noah said what he said next, which was even more shocking.

'We should eat our stash,' he said.

'Our stash' meant our stash of sweets, kept in a black shoe box. We'd collected them over a few months. They were supposed to be for emergencies, like if there was a war or something. Eating our stash was very symbolic, which is when one thing stands for another thing and it means more than you think at first.

The big box of sweets, hidden in a hole in the floor covered over with a piece of carpet, was sort of the soul of the Gang. As long as it was still there, the Gang was still alive. Without it the Gang was like a dead body. The stash of sweets was even more important than the den. We could always build another den, but when our sweets were gone, well, that was it, they were gone. Unless we bought some more, that is.

With a heavy heart I moved the carpet and got the box out of the hole. Everyone gathered round as I opened the lid. We all looked at the pile of goodies. Whenever we bought some sweets, we were meant to save something to put in the box. I suppose we all cheated a bit, because it's quite hard not to just eat all your sweets when you buy them, but the box was still pretty full. With the shiny wrappers and gold paper, it looked like a box of pirate treasure.

I shared them out. It had looked like a pretty good stash when you saw them all together in the box, but when it was split between the four of us, it didn't seem that much. Just a couple of handfuls of chews and fruit pastilles and broken-up blocks of chocolate and not even a whole packet of crisps each.

That was symbolic too. The Gang was like the stash of sweets. Quite impressive all together, but a bit rubbish when you looked at the separate parts.

Still, eating sweets always cheers you up a bit, and we even began to think that, with Luke and Oliver and Carl on our side, we might have a chance of beating the old estate kids.

It was then that we heard the rapping of a stick on the outside of the den. Bad news, we all thought. And we were right.

Chapter Thirteen

THE TRAITOR IN OUR MIDST

'Who is it?' I shouted.

'Me,' said a voice we knew all too well.

'Oh no,' groaned The Moan. 'What does *she* want?'

'Probably to rub salt in our wounds,' said Noah.

We all crawled outside to see.

Jennifer was there, holding a big stick. I thought for a second that her plan was to whack us with it, probably as a way of making us weak for the Big Match, like when Delilah cut off Samson's hair so he became rubbish at fighting, which is a story we did in R.E. Up until then Samson was really cool, and slayed – which means killed – about a million Philistines, who were the baddies, with various weapons, including his bare hands and the jaw bone of an ass, which is a donkey and not your bum.

I walked forward to talk to her, as I was still the Leader for the time being. I kept an eye on her stick, in case she made a sudden swipe.

'What do you want, Jennifer?'

Her hair wasn't in its usual volcano shape today, and it actually looked quite normal. It went down instead of up, which, if you ask me, is the right way for hair to go.

She threw her stick into the bushes. At first, when I saw her hand move, I thought she was going to whip me with it, so I stepped back, which wasn't very cool. But if there's one lesson I've learned in life it's that you can't be cool all the time.

'You know Carl?' she said.

'Of course we know Carl. He's playing in our team today, so we should know him.'

'He isn't.'

'Isn't what?'

'Playing in your team today. Or ever, probably.'

I found it hard to understand her face. I didn't know if she was enjoying this, or was actually trying to help us.

There were cries of surprise and alarm from the boys behind me.

'What do you mean?' I said. 'He *is* playing for us. He came to our practice – I mean training session – yesterday. He's our best player.'

'It's all a trick,' said Jennifer.

'What?' I replied, but I was beginning to have a rotten feeling inside me even before Jennifer answered.

'He's only pretending to be on your team. It's all so Dockery can find out what your plans are, and when you all turn up at three o'clock, Carl's going to go and play for

Dockery's team. And it means you'll only have six players, and they'll have seven.'

'The evil sneaky swine,' said Jamie. 'I knew it was too good to be true.'

'They'll know all about our Christmas tree,' said The Moan.

'You're not lying, are you, Jennifer?' I asked, but I knew it was true. Everything started to fall into place.

'I do not tell lies,' she answered, sounding very high and mighty.

'That's true, she doesn't,' said The Moan, but he didn't mean it as a compliment. 'She never covers for me when I'm in trouble.'

I glanced around at the boys. They looked really, really depressed about this news.

'Let's say it's true then. But how do you know about it?'

'My friend Sarah is friends with his sister's friend, Fiona.'

'Eh?'

'I just heard, OK?'

'Why are you telling us this? Is it because you want to gloat?'

'No.'

'Ha!' said The Moan. 'She doesn't even know what gloat means.'

'I do so, stupid boy! It means being happy that someone else is sad, and then you make fun of them. And no, that isn't why I'm telling you.'

'Why then?'

'They were going to cheat. I didn't think it was fair. Especially as they're all bigger than you anyway. I hate things that aren't fair.'

'That's really nice of you, Jennifer,' I said. And I meant it. 'I'm really sorry about . . . you know.'

'Are you?'

'Yeah. I should never have made you show us your bare bum. I should just have said there were no girls allowed.'

'But why are there no girls allowed?'

'Why? But . . . but . . . I don't know, really.'

I was going to say that stuff about girls tidying up your den and making your action figures wear frilly dresses, but I realized that Jennifer wasn't that kind of girl. In fact, for all I knew for sure, there weren't any girls who would do all that.

I looked round for support from my gang, but they were all hanging their heads. I could understand why.

'What are you going to do about the game?' Jennifer asked after a while. She'd probably got bored with waiting for me to say something.

'Well, we can either not turn up, or play anyway, with six men.'

Jennifer started laughing. 'Six men! Ha, you mean six boys.'

'You always say "men" in teams. You'd probably say men even if you had girls.'

'And you can't get anyone else to play?'

'Too late now.'

Jennifer was looking at me in a funny way.

Then I had one of my ideas. It was probably the craziest idea I'd ever had, and that was saying something.

I turned to the Gang. 'We need to have a talk in the den,' I said to them. Then I turned again to Jennifer.

'Wait here a minute, will you?' I said it in my nicest voice.

Chapter Fourteen

THE KISS

'What's all this about?' asked Noah when we were inside.

'I'm going to ask her.'

'Ask who?' said Jamie.

'Jennifer.'

'Ask her what?' said The Moan.

'If she wants to play.'

'WHAAAAAAT!' The shout came from all of them together.

'Look,' I said, 'we haven't got anyone else. And she looks quite sporty. Have you seen her doing cartwheels?'

'But cartwheels aren't allowed in football,'

said The Moan.

'It's just an example. She might be one of those girls who are really good at football. I saw a film about them once.'

'Yeah,' said Jamie thoughtfully. 'I saw that. She runs fast too. And running *is* allowed in football. In fact it's, erm, the opposite of not allowed . . .'

'Compulsory,' said Noah.

'Yeah, that,' said Jamie.

'She's your sister, Phillip,' said Noah. 'Is she good at sport?'

'Well,' said The Moan reluctantly, 'she's in lots of sports clubs. She goes off to do stuff almost every evening. I don't pay much attention to it. But yes, actually, I think she *is* sporty. When she throws things at me, she usually hits the target.'

'There's another thing,' I said. 'I feel really rotten about what we did to her . . .'

'What *we* did?' said Noah.

'OK, what *I* did. And this way we get a player who might actually be quite good, and I can sort of say sorry to her.'

'But do we really want a girl in our team?' said Phillip. 'Especially if she's my sister?'

'In life you don't always get exactly what you want,' I said. 'Sometimes you have to do something because it's right, even when you don't really want to.'

There was nothing much more to be said, and, anyway, just then Jennifer shouted from outside, 'I'm going home.'

'Hang on,' I shouted back, and we all crawled out again.

Jennifer was waiting for us. 'What were you talking about?' she asked.

'Well, er, you, basically.'

'Oh.'

'We'd like to ask you something.'

'What? It better not be to do with showing my bum.'

'No, it's nothing to do with that. If you want to, you can play in our football team.'

'That's not really a question.'

I sighed. Jennifer wasn't making this easy.

'OK then, will you play in our football team?'

'Say please.'

'Please.'

'No.'

'No?'

'No. Not unless you say how sorry you are.'

'I've already said sorry.'

'Say it again.'

'I'm really sorry for what I did.'

'And you have to give me a kiss.'

'WHAT!'

'A kiss.'

'That's definitely not fair.'

Then I heard Noah behind me say, 'Go on, Ludo. You've gone this far. It won't kill you.'

I think the boys might have been enjoying this.

'All right then,' I said miserably, 'but not on the lips.'

'Yuck, no. On the cheek.'

'You don't mean your bum cheek, do you? Because if you do, you can just forget it and the whole deal is off.'

'You are *so* immature. No, not on my bottom, although that would be what I believe is called poetic justice. I mean here, on my face.'

She pointed to her left cheek. Someone pushed me from behind. I walked slowly forwards, aiming my lips exactly where she had pointed. I didn't want her to say I'd done it in the wrong place so she could make me kiss her again. But as I stepped forward I put my foot in a Smarties-tube fart-bomb trap, so a horrible smell came out at the same time as the kiss, which actually landed on her arm, because I'd half fallen into the hole, and that all led to quite a lot of commotion, with Jennifer pulling away, going 'Poooooooooohhhh,' and the boys all rolling about laughing, and me collapsing on the floor.

But then Jennifer came back and helped me up, saying, 'Good trap,' and we all sort of laughed together, not anyone laughing at anyone else, but all of us laughing at everything.

Chapter Fifteen

THE TRAITOR UNMASKED

At five to three we all met at the pitch. Only Phillip had a real football kit; the rest of us were wearing ordinary white T-shirts and shorts, but I still think we all looked pretty good. I was surprised to see that there were quite a lot of spectators, maybe thirty kids.

Amazingly, Mrs Cake was there as well, with Trixie. Trixie was on a lead, but she still kept leaping up trying to bite the nearest child. I don't suppose there was a lot of excitement in Mrs Cake's life, so watching some little kids get kicked around by some slightly bigger kids probably counted as entertainment to her.

Anyway, having a big crowd there to watch piled even more pressure on me. I'd never played in front of a crowd before. None of us had.

Jennifer was standing there with some of her friends. She was wearing a pink tracksuit, which was pretty bad,

but I suppose it was the only one she owned.

The Dockery team were kicking the ball around. Just as I suspected, there were six of them. There was Dockery, Stanton, Furbank, Larkin (dribbling and drooling at the same time), and the two others whose names I could never remember. They all had proper kit. They even had

shin pads. That seemed a bit strange to me – *we* were going to get kicked, but *they* had the shin pads! I suppose there's always a chance that when you try to kick someone, you might get it a bit wrong and hit them with your shin instead, so they were probably guarding against that. I imagined their mums sending them off to play, saying, 'Do be careful, dear, when you kick those little children. Make sure you don't hurt yourselves.' They were laughing a lot (the Dockery Gang, I mean, not their mums), and generally looking smug.

Carl was standing by himself near the halfway line, wearing a white T-shirt. But there was something odd about it. It was too chunky and wrinkled. He looked smug as well, or rather like someone trying not to look smug, but failing. I think they were waiting till the last minute to take maximum advantage of the trick, trying to make us look as stupid as possible.

Well, this time the trick was going to be turned back on them.

I marched straight up to Carl. He started to say something, but I spoke over him in a loud voice so that everyone could hear – the rest of the Dockery Gang plus all the kids watching.

'You're sacked,' I said.

'B-b-but . . .'

'I'm sorry, but we've decided you're not good enough to play in our team. In fact you're completely rubbish. And your hair looks stupid. We've got someone good to play instead of you.'

'You can't sack me, because I'm . . . I mean, I was . . . I mean . . .'

But I'd already turned my back on him and gone to rejoin my team. We all looked towards the sideline, knowing that the eyes of the Dockery Gang as well as the crowd would follow us. Then I waved to Jennifer, who, grinning from ear to ear, took off her track suit and ran out to join us.

Underneath the horrible pink tracksuit she was wearing a proper white football kit that used to belong to Phillip, and she looked really good. I'd warned her against doing any cartwheels, but I think she probably knew that already. She ran so fast her feet hardly seemed to touch the ground.

I looked at the opposition. They didn't know what to think about Jennifer. You could see from their faces that they wanted to laugh, but there was also something a bit like fear in their eyes. They could see that Jennifer was fast and sporty, and I reckon they were imagining what everyone would say if they got beat by a team with a girl in it.

Then Dockery stepped forward. 'No girls allowed!' he shouted.

'Says who?' I shouted back. 'We never said anything about girls playing or not playing, so that means they can. If you're afraid to play us, then fine. We win.'

There was a sort of murmur from the crowd then. I think they saw that we were being fair and Dockery wasn't.

Dockery clamped his mouth shut after that. Carl was still hovering about, unsure what to do or where to go. 'Come on then,' Dockery shouted at him. 'Sort your kit out.'

Then Carl took off his white shirt and underneath it he was wearing a blue one.

The crowd laughed at that, and someone shouted out, 'Cheats', but when Dockery went over towards them, most of the kids went quiet. They were still scared of him. And so was I.

Chapter Sixteen

THE BIG MATCH

Noah, Oliver, Luke, Jamie, The Moan and Jennifer gathered round while I gave them a last quick team talk.

'Let's try to pass the ball. And if we can, we should probably try to score. Oh, and we should try to stop them from scoring. If we can score more goals than them, then I think we've got a good chance of winning. Any questions?'

There weren't any. I then got them all to stand in their positions. Jennifer was going to be our lone striker, taking Carl's place.

The opposition lined up in their half. My heart was racing. They all looked so big and strong, and we looked so weak and feeble, especially little Luke and Oliver, who were three years younger than most of the kids in Dockery's team. It felt like we were up against a gang of giants and ogres and trolls.

Someone shouted out, 'OK, let's go,' and the next thing we knew they were all charging towards us. They hadn't bothered with a proper kick-off. We weren't even ready. Carl passed the ball to Dockery, who ran down the middle of the pitch towards our goal. Luke tried to tackle him, but Dockery just shoved him aside. I shouted 'Foul' and 'Free kick' but they didn't stop. Noah tried to get to him, but he wasn't fast enough. Then Dockery was right in front of our goal, with just Jamie in the way. Jamie's legs were shaking, and he held his hands and the gloves with the wrong fingers out in front of him. Dockery could have easily slid the ball past him into the net, but he decided to blast it.

And blast it he did, right into Jamie's face. It bounced away and went out for a corner.

It must have hurt like mad, but Jamie didn't cry, which made me really proud.

There were complaints from some of Dockery's team, but he silenced them with a glare. Larkin took the corner. I managed to get to it first and blindly whacked up the pitch, just trying to get it out of the danger zone.

I didn't aim for her, but it turned into a brilliant pass to Jennifer.

All of the Dockery team except for the goalkeeper had come up into our half for the corner. The ball bounced ahead of Jennifer, rolling slowly towards their goal. She leaped after it like a racehorse. Boy, but she looked fantastic, her white kit gleaming in the sun.

Their goalie, William Stanton, didn't

know whether to come out to meet her or stay in his goal. The ball rolled on and Jennifer chased it down. No, not like a racehorse or a gazelle or anything like that, but like a predator, a cheetah.

We held our breath. The Dockery Gang held their breath. The crowd held their breath. The tension hummed in the air like an electric storm.

She was almost there now, with the ball rolling slowly, almost coming to a stop about four metres from the goal. Jennifer slowed, steadied herself and drew back her foot for what was going to be an almighty shot, a real net-breaker, a rocket, a thunderbolt.

She swung.

You could hear it as well as see it. A *whoosh* as her foot cut through the air at the speed of sound.

And she completely missed the ball.

Missed the ball, flew into the air and landed smack on her bottom on a patch of bare mud.

I held my head in my hands.

The Moan moaned.

Jamie said, 'That was rubbish.'

Even Noah let out a little gasp of despair.

The enemy laughed like a pack of hyenas. The crowd joined in with them. Trixie barked.

We'd made a terrible, terrible mistake. Jennifer might be sporty, but whatever sports she was sporty at, football wasn't one of them.

So now not only did we have a girl on the team, we had a useless girl.

Jennifer sat there, looking more annoyed than embarrassed, as if she blamed the ground or the ball for the fact that she'd missed it by a mile.

Stanton jogged up and booted the ball down the pitch. That's it, I thought, it's going to be carnage. And in a strange way, that turned out to be right.

Out of the corner of my eye I could still

see Jennifer sitting in the patch of mud. I thought she might stay there for the rest of the game, but she was so rubbish at football I didn't think it really mattered.

Dockery had the ball, thundering along on his massive legs, charging towards our goal. There was no way he was going to miss again. But then little Luke somehow managed to poke the ball out from under his feet. It rolled to The Moan. Dockery looked surprised as well as furious at being tackled. You could see that he thought about kicking Luke, but then decided he might as well kick The Moan, which meant he'd have the ball again. In fact he didn't even bother kicking him – he just ran over, grabbed his shirt and threw him on the ground. You couldn't get a more obvious bit of nasty cheating.

And then I saw a blur. The blur moved from where Jennifer had been sitting in the mud. It flashed all the way down the pitch to where Dockery was standing. Then the blur became clearer, and I saw that it was Jennifer.

Her face had the look of a warrior princess: grim, determined, fatal.

She ran straight at Dockery, flew into the air and landed an amazing kick right in the middle of his chest, shouting out, 'Hiiiiiiii-yahhhhh!'

Dockery staggered back, a look of amazement on his face. Then Jennifer followed it up with two more kung-fu-style kicks, and Dockery was on the floor.

'Don't you dare touch my brother!' she screamed.

Carl lumbered up to help his chief, but Jennifer got him too, with a chop to the arm. And then she chased James Furbank, and tripped him up and pushed his face into the mud.

Then I realized what it was that Jennifer was sporty at. The Moan said she was always off at clubs in the evening. I looked at him (he was still sitting on the floor, where Dockery had pushed him). He was grinning.

'Karate!' we said together, and laughed.

And now the whole crowd were laughing too. Jennifer, the little pocket warrior, was chasing all the Dockery Gang around the pitch. She kept landing kicks and punches, and they were squealing and yelling. Finally she chased them all off the pitch, and then Mrs Cake let Trixie off her lead, and she joined Jennifer in the attack, biting at heels and bottoms, and the whole Dockery Gang kept on running until they were out of sight.

The rest of our team were cheering like mad by now. Even The Moan, who hated to admit that Jennifer had ever done anything right.

Finally Jennifer came back and stood with us. She was smiling sheepishly – not that sheep really smile, but you know what I mean.

'Well, Jennifer,' I said, trying to keep a straight face. 'I can't say I approve of that sort of thing. We were supposed to be here to play football, and you turned it into a kung fu movie.'

'It was tae kwon do, actually,' she said. 'I'm a red belt. They don't let you go any higher until you're fifteen.'

'Well, whatever, but it's not really the sort of thing we do in our gang,' I said, still trying not to grin. But I couldn't keep it up. A smile sneaked onto my face, and then completely took over, and soon I was laughing again with the rest as we went over what Jennifer had done, and I pretended to be Dockery, blubbing like a big fat baby.

Finally I said, 'I don't suppose we'll be bothered much by that lot for a while.'

Then Jamie said, 'But we haven't won the game yet. It's still nil–nil.'

'You're right,' I replied. 'Do you want to go and blast one in, Jenny? You've earned it.'

'Um, no, maybe I should let someone else do it. I don't know where it might end up. I'm much better at kicking people than balls.'

Well, that was certainly true. So I decided that I should be the one. I dribbled the ball up the pitch by myself, until I was a couple of metres from the goal, and then I kicked it with all my might. It whistled in, and the few people still there cheered loudly. One of them was Mrs Cake, who'd put Trixie back on her lead. She walked over to us.

'I've got something for you boys.'

We didn't know what it was going to be.

Perhaps she was going to set Trixie on us, now she'd got her breath back from chasing Dockery halfway to London.

'I was going to share them with your friends, but as they've run away, you might as well have them all to yourselves.'

And then she gave us a huge bag of mixed sweets, with chocolates, chews, fruit pastilles, jelly sweets, *everything*. It was almost as much as we'd had in our stash.

I made everyone say thank you properly, and then she went back to her bungalow, dragging Trixie with her. It turned out that Mrs Cake wasn't such an old witch after all, unless she'd poisoned the sweets or sucked all the goodness out of them, but that was a chance I was prepared to take.

'OK, you lot, back to the den,' I said. 'We can eat half of these, and put the rest in the shoe box ready for the next emergency. The Gang is saved.'

'What about me?' said Jennifer as we began the walk to the woods.

'You, Jenny? Well, you're one of us now. One of the Bare Bum Gang. It began as an insult, but now I think we should sing it out loud.'

And we all did.

'*Watch out, people, here we come,*
We are the Gang with the big bare bum.
Ring that bell, clang clang clang,
That's why we're called the Bare Bum Gang.
We're like something off the telly,
We're all bare and we're all smelly!'

Supplementary material, chiefly concerning the manufacture of fart bombs, and the making of traps. And also dens.

Making a Smarties-tube Fart Bomb

The hardest part of making a Smarties-tube fart bomb is getting the farts in the first place. There are two main ways of doing this. The first is just to wait around until one comes along. Although this can be boring, you have to remain alert at all times in case you miss it. While you are waiting for one to come, you could do something else as well.

I suggest the following:

Make a model aeroplane. Although the Spitfire is the best ever fighter aircraft, you might decide that a Hurricane is better when waiting for a fart, as a Hurricane is also a kind of mighty wind.

Throw stones – but not at other children, or animals, except for ones that are attacking you – for example, bears, leopards, giant eagles or octopuses. Aim instead at things that don't have feelings, like trees, puddles and girls. Only joking. DO NOT THROW STONES AT GIRLS – they'll tell on you and you won't be allowed to watch *Dr Who*

If you don't want to just wait for a fart to arrive, you can force it to come by eating special food. As is known by everyone, beans are best for this. Any type of bean will do, except for Mexican jumping beans, which aren't technically a bean at all, but a type of worm. Don't waste your money on fart sweets from joke shops because I've tried them and they don't work.

The next most difficult thing is getting the fart into the Smarties tube. Some people think this is best done in the bath, where you simply put the tube over the bubbles. However, a more scientific answer is to use some proper equipment. I have designed a fart-catching apparatus, which I can now reveal.

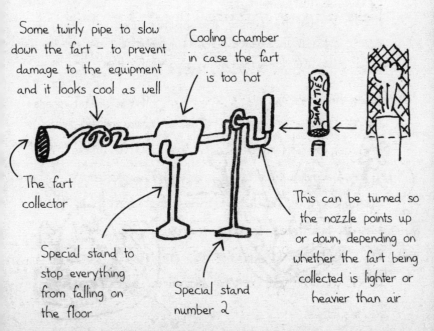

Some twirly pipe to slow down the fart – to prevent damage to the equipment and it looks cool as well

Cooling chamber in case the fart is too hot

The fart collector

Special stand to stop everything from falling on the floor

Special stand number 2

This can be turned so the nozzle points up or down, depending on whether the fart being collected is lighter or heavier than air

Once you have loaded the tube, you next make the trap. Dig a hole in the ground. You can use sharp sticks for that, or borrow a spade. Not a toy spade like you use on the beach, because that will probably break, and then you'll have to hide it and pretend you didn't know what happened to it when you next go to the seaside. Put the tubes in the hole. Put some twigs over the hole and then some grass over the twigs. It is now invisible, and all you have to do is wait for someone to set it off.

This is what happens then:

To Make a Smarties-tube Fart bomb trap
1. Get some Smarties tubes
2. Get some farts
3. Put the farts in the smarties tubes
4. Put the loaded bomb in a hole
5. Wait for somebody to step in the hole

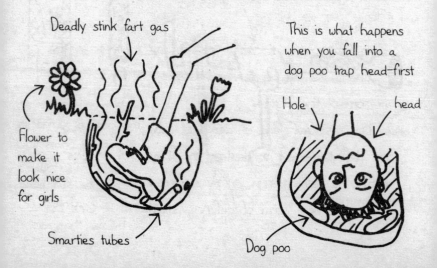

Deadly stink fart gas

Flower to make it look nice for girls

Smarties tubes

This is what happens when you fall into a dog poo trap head-first

Hole

head

Dog poo

As you'll see, I've also included a picture of a dog-poo trap, which is an even nastier version of the Smarties-tube fart-bomb trap. Usually people don't fall in headfirst, but they might and it would serve them right if they did, for trying to sneak up on our den.

Making a den

The den is the most important thing about having a gang. You can make a den out of almost anything. However dens made out of newspaper, cardboard, tissue paper or cotton wool will be rubbish, especially when it rains.

Much will depend on where and when you are building your den. In the North Pole, your den will probably be an igloo made out of snow. In the Wild West your den will usually be a wigwam or possibly a tepee. In the Olden Days, your den would probably have been a small castle, made out of stone. In the future there will be dens in outer space and at the bottom of the ocean.

But whatever kind of den you have, your enemies will definitely want to destroy it. They can do this either by kicking it in, or by weeing in it. Some people think the best form of defence is attack. In fact the best form of defence is running away. However, dens cannot run away. The best form of defence for a den is hiding. You should therefore hide your den by covering it in leaves, wood, soil, newspaper, plastic bags or army camouflage netting. Our den is hidden under a weeping willow tree, and half of it is a sort of cave dug into the side of a hill.

Unfortunately sometimes your enemies will find your den. That is when the traps come in handy.

Every good den will have a secret stash of sweets hidden in it. If there is a siege lasting months or years, you can eat your special stash of sweets to stay alive.